John Prater

"No!" said Joe

WALKER BOOKS
AND SUBSIDIARIES

LONDON • BOSTON • SYDNEY

"Joe, fetch your coat, your gloves and hat,
Then find your other shoe,
We need to get some shopping done
And you are coming too."

"No," said Joe.

THIS WALKER BOOK BELONGS TO:

_____

_____

_____

_____

For Joel and Holly

First published 1991 by Walker Books Ltd
87 Vauxhall Walk, London SE11 5HJ

This edition published 1996

2 4 6 8 10 9 7 5 3 1

© 1991 John Prater

Printed in Hong Kong

This book has been typeset in Garamond Light.

British Library Cataloguing in Publication Data
A catalogue record for this book is
available from the British Library.

ISBN 0-7445-4718-0

"Now don't be silly and make a fuss,
I know you want to play,
But we must get the shopping done,
There's lots to do today."

"No," said Joe.

"Oh, come on, Joe, you naughty boy,
If you behave this way,
I think we'll ask the Wicked Witch
To take you far away."

"Yes," said Joe.

"She'll make you eat disgusting things,
Like snake and spider stew,
Or slug and worm spaghetti –
Is that all right with you?"

"Yes," said Joe.

"And then she'll cast a dreadful spell:
You'll end up as a bat,
Or maybe as a slimy toad,
Now, what do you think of that?"

"Yes," said Joe.

"Perhaps she'll soon get tired of you
And stuff you in a sack,
Then give you to a passing Giant
Who'll never bring you back."

"Yes," said Joe.

"He'll scoop you up and take you home
To scare you as he reads
All through the dark and fearsome night
Of dreadful giant deeds."

"Yes," said Joe.

"He might decide to have a treat
And grind you to a pulp,
Then cook you in a great big pie
To swallow in one gulp."

"Yes," said Joe.

"Or else perhaps he'll leave you
At a haunted house he knows,
Where floorboards creak, shutters squeak,
And no one ever goes."

"Yes," said Joe.

"The ghosts inside are wild and mad,
With glowing eyes that stare.
They hide in cupboards, walk through walls
And spook you everywhere."

"Yes," said Joe.

"They gather in a ghastly gang,
And swoop and wail and moan;
There isn't anyone alive
Who'll stay in there alone."

"Yes," said Joe.

"Well, really, Joe, you are so brave,
There's nothing more to say.
We'll just drive off and leave you here
All by yourself to play."

"NO!" said Joe.

"Oh, you know we didn't mean it,
We'd never, ever go.
Come and have a special hug,
A big hug just for Joe.
Now get your coat, your gloves and hat,
And there's the missing shoe,
We'll quickly get the shopping done
Then buy a treat for you."

"YES!" said Joe.

MORE WALKER PAPERBACKS
For You to Enjoy

ONCE UPON A TIME
by Vivian French/John Prater

A little boy tells of his "dull" day, while all around a host of favourite nursery characters act out their stories.

"The pictures are excellent, the telegraphic text perfect, the idea brilliant.
We have here a classic, I'm sure, with an author-reader bond
as strong as *Rosie's Walk.*" *Books for Keeps*

0-7445-3690-1   £4.99

THE GREATEST SHOW ON EARTH
by John Prater

Everyone in the circus can perform amazing feats – except, it seems, poor Harry…
But there's a twist in the tail of this entertaining big-top romp.

"John Prater's has been one of the exciting arrivals on the picture-book scene in recent years…
A wide page and bold colour push the story along with much gusto." *The Junior Bookshelf*

0-7445-4359-2   £4.99

WILLY THE WIMP
WILLY THE CHAMP
by Anthony Browne

Two popular tales about the mild chimp, who may look a wimp
but somehow always comes out on top! "Made me laugh out loud." *Parents*

Willy the Wimp   0-7445-4363-0   £4.50
Willy the Champ   0-7445-4356-8   £4.99

Walker Paperbacks are available from most booksellers, or by post from B.B.C.S., P.O. Box 941, Hull, North Humberside HU1 3YQ
24 hour telephone credit card line 01482 224626

To order, send: Title, author, ISBN number and price for each book ordered, your full name and address,
cheque or postal order payable to BBCS for the total amount and allow the following for postage and packing:
UK and BFPO: £1.00 for the first book, and 50p for each additional book to a maximum of £3.50.
Overseas and Eire: £2.00 for the first book, £1.00 for the second and 50p for each additional book.

Prices and availability are subject to change without notice.